EAST HADDAM FREE PUBLIC LIBRARY
18 PLAINS RD. P.O. BOX 372
MOODUS, CONNECTICUT 06469

For Ella, with love – *AM*

For Missy – *JC*

Text copyright © 2003 by Angela McAllister
Illustrations copyright © 2003 by Jason Cockcroft

All rights reserved. No part of this book may be used or reproduced
in any manner whatsoever without written permission from
the publisher except in the case of brief quotations
embodied in critical articles or reviews.

Published by Bloomsbury, New York and London
Bloomsbury USA Children's Books
175 Fifth Avenue
New York, New York 10010

Library of Congress Cataloging-in-Publication Data
McAllister, Angela.
The Little Blue Rabbit / by Angela McAllister; illustrated by Jason Cockcroft. p. cm.
Summary: Sad when his boy suddenly disappears, a stuffed toy rabbit is
comforted by the other toys until his boy finally returns.
ISBN 1-58234-834-0 (alk. paper)
[1. Toys—Fiction. 2. Rabbits—Fiction.] I. Cockcroft, Jason, ill. II. Title.
PZ7.M11714 Li 2003
[E]—dc21
2002034151

First U. S. Edition 2003
Printed in China by South China Printing Company, Dongguan, Guangdong
3 5 7 9 10 8 6 4 2

The Little Blue Rabbit

EAST HADDAM FREE PUBLIC LIBRARY
18 PLAINS RD. P.O. BOX 372
MOODUS, CONNECTICUT 06469

DISCARD

by Angela McAllister
illustrated by Jason Cockcroft

BLOOMSBURY
CHILDREN'S
BOOKS

Blue Rabbit slept in a very big bed with a very big pillow.
He couldn't reach the bottom with his toes. He couldn't
reach the top with the tips of his ears.
But Blue Rabbit didn't feel lost in the very big bed
because every night he had his Boy to cuddle.

Boy always understood if Blue Rabbit was worried or sad.
Boy always helped if Blue Rabbit was puzzled or stuck.
Boy was soft and warm and stuffed with love, and each night
they fell asleep together in the very big bed.

But one evening Blue Rabbit couldn't find his Boy.
"Where did you see him last?" asked the toys.
Blue Rabbit couldn't remember. "He was here
this morning and now he's lost."

The toys agreed to help. They hunted in all the usual places. Then they hunted in unusual places. But Boy was nowhere to be found.

The house grew dark and the toys grew sleepy.
"Don't worry," they said, "he'll turn up tomorrow."

For the first time Blue Rabbit's big bed felt cold and lonely. He climbed in and pulled the covers up to his chin. "I can't go to sleep without my Boy," he said in a small voice.

Creepy shadows darted across the ceiling. Night noises teased and tricked. Blue Rabbit thought he heard something rustle under the bed. He didn't feel brave without his Boy, but he had to look …

Slowly, holding on to the very big pillow, he tried to peer under the bed. Further and further he stretched until …

... out he fell with a bump!

A mouse scampered up. "Have you seen my Boy?" asked Blue Rabbit.
But the mouse just shook her head and ran away.

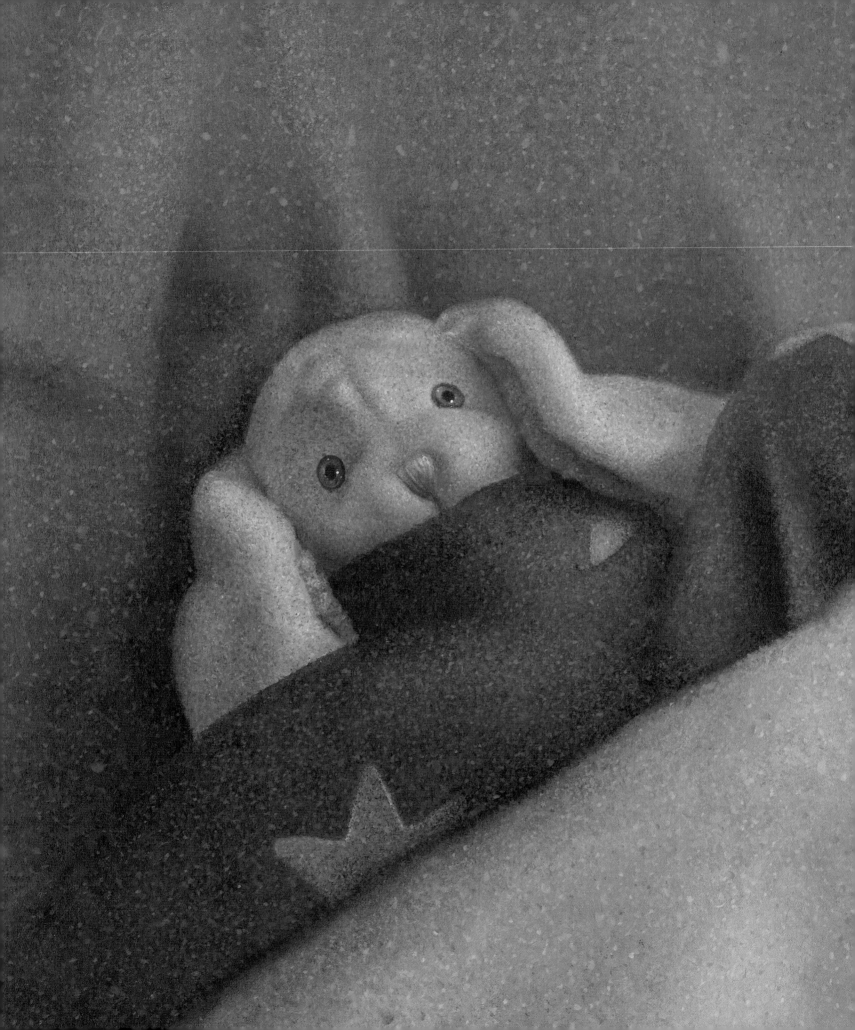

Blue Rabbit climbed back into bed.
He told himself a story but he
couldn't get to sleep without his
Boy. So he sat up all night long,
closing first one eye and then the
other until morning.

Once more Blue Rabbit's whiskers bristled and his eyes sparkled. Could it really be true? Boy was different somehow … Boy had turned a rusty brown color and his clothes had all shrunk. "I suppose he must have been left out in the garden, in the rain," thought Blue Rabbit.

But when they hugged each other tight,
Blue Rabbit knew his Boy hadn't really
changed at all. For he was still soft and
warm and stuffed with love.